This book is for:

....

because I like you *very* much.

Copyright © 2007 by Harmen van Straaten
First published in Holland under the title *Eendje voor jou*
by Leopold, Amsterdam.
English translation copyright © 2007 by
North-South Books Inc., New York.

First published in the United States, Great Britain, Canada,
Australia, and New Zealand in 2007 by North-South Books Inc.,
an imprint of NordSüd Verlag AG, Zürich, Switzerland.
Distributed in the United States by North-South Books Inc., New York.

Library of Congress Cataloging-in-Publication Data is available.
A CIP catalogue record for this book is available from The British Library.

ISBN-13: 978-0-7358-2163-7 / ISBN-10: 0-7358-2163-1 (trade edition)
10 9 8 7 6 5 4 3 2 1

Printed in Belgium

www.northsouth.com

Harmen van Straaten

For Me?

Translated by MaryChris Bradley

NorthSouth
BOOKS
New York / London

Quickly, Duck ripped open the envelope.
Inside was a red rose and a piece of paper with
an enormous red heart on it, but no signature.
Duck was very surprised. "For me?" he wondered.
Perhaps Toad would know . . .

Duck ran all the way to Toad's house.
"I got a rose and a heart!" he said,
panting. That's when he noticed that
Otter and Hedgehog were already there,
and all three of them were holding roses!

"So did we!" they all said.

"What do you think it means?"
asked Duck.

"Maybe it means that one of us is
in love," suggested Toad.

"Oh!" Otter replied. "Are you in love
with me?"

"Not really," said Toad, "I like you,
Otter, but . . . "

"Perhaps it's someone we don't know," said
Hedgehog anxiously.

"I wonder who it could be," said Duck.

"I'd like to know, too," said Toad.

"Hmmm, you smell very nice today, Toad," teased Duck. "Are you in love with someone?"

"Not I," said Toad.
"But look at Otter fixing
his hair. He must be the
one in love!"

"I know, I'm going to write a poem for my love, whoever she is," Toad declared.

"How do you know that she is in love with you?" asked Otter. "I got the first letter. Perhaps it's me that she's in love with!"

"But I got the biggest rose," said Hedgehog. "That means I'm the one!"

"No it doesn't, I'm the one!" yelled Toad.

"You don't think I'm going to give up just like that, do you?" asked Otter angrily.

"Wait, wait, let's not fight about this," interrupted Duck. He picked up one of the roses and pulled off a petal. "She loves me," he said softly. He passed the flower to Toad. "Now it's your turn," he said. "Whoever picks the last petal is the one she loves."

Toad closed his eyes and pulled off a petal. "She loves me, only me," he whispered softly. Slowly he handed the rose to Otter, who took his turn. The rose went from hand to hand. Soon there were more petals on the floor than on the rose.

No one noticed that someone had quietly
come in.

"Ahem," coughed that someone.

Everyone turned around.

"Hi, I'm Mole," she said. "I'm your new neighbor. Did you all get my messages? I wanted to meet you, but I'm a little shy . . ."

"So *you* sent us these?" they asked, holding out their roses.

"Yes," replied Mole, "I did."

"Ahhh," said Duck. "Then they really *were* for all of us. Why didn't you write anything on the paper?"

"Well, I'm not very good with words," replied Mole.

"I could have read it—I have reading glasses," said Toad proudly, adjusting his glasses.

"Humph!" muttered Otter. Toad was always showing off. "Well, I have a boat!" he shouted. "I could take you for a boat ride!"

"Will we all fit?" asked Mole.

"If we all sit close together," said Hedgehog. "Mole, you can sit next to me."

So the five of them climbed into Otter's boat. It was a very tight fit!

"Where should we go?" asked Otter.

"I know," said Duck, "let's go to my house. We can make dinner for our new friend!"

"That sounds wonderful!" laughed Mole.

They spent the whole day together. When evening came, they were still on the deck at Duck's house. Duck was playing the accordion while Otter, Hedgehog, and Mole took turns singing.

Mole yawned a little. "I'm getting tired," she said.

"We'll take you home," said Otter.

Duck cleared his throat. "There's something I want to say before you go," he said. "Thank you for the flower. And here's one for you, Mole, my new friend."

"Why, thank you, Duck!" replied Mole. "And thanks to all my new friends. I like you all *very* much!"

"Good-bye! Come back soon!" Duck called as they floated away.

"Thanks again! See you soon," Mole called back.

Happy, Duck went to bed. His whole house smelled like roses, but best of all, he had a new friend . . .